North American

Withdrawn

Song of a Wolf

At daybreak
I roam
galloping
I roam.

At daybreak
I roam
trotting
I roam.

At daybreak
I roam.
In a timid manner
I roam.

At daybreak
I roam
watching cautiously
I roam.

Author's Note

This myth comes from the Algonquin Indians of
the north east U.S.A.

A *fisher* is a small animal (like an ermine) that once
thrived in the cold climates of the northern USA and
Canada. It has been hunted to near extinction for its
beautiful and valuable fur.

The fisher stars are known to us as the plough.

Copyright © Joanna Troughton, 1992
First published in 1992 by
Blackie Children's Books
27 Wrights Lane, London, W8 5TZ, England
A CIP catalogue record for this book is available
from The British Library

ISBN 0-216-93200-9

First American edition published in 1992 by
Peter Bedrick Books
2112 Broadway
New York, NY 10023

Library of Congress Cataloging-in-Publication Data
is available for this title.

ISBN 0-87226-464-5

Printed in Hong Kong

Folk Tales of the World

How the Seasons Came

A North American Indian Folk Tale

Retold and illustrated by

Joanna Troughton

Blackie
London

Bedrick/Blackie
New York

This is how it has always been told.
The wolf's son fell ill, and no one
could cure him.

'It is the cold,' said the fisher, who was
the wolf's friend. For in those days it
was winter all the year round.

The fisher had heard that the weather
was warmer in the land above the sky.

'If we could find a way to the Land Above,
maybe we could bring some warmth back to
earth, and then your son would be well again.'

All the animals tried to help.

But none could jump high enough.

Until the fisher tried. He was long and thin. He jumped so high that he made a hole in the sky, through to the land above.

Then the wolf jumped, and followed his
friend the fisher to the land above. It was
warm and sunny there. They found
themselves on a broad plain. On the plain
were lodges. At the doorways of three of
these lodges hung cages, each with a
beautiful bird. And all the birds were
singing.

The Song of the Spring Bird

Out of the earth
I sing for them.
The tall grasses
I sing for them.
Out of the sky
I sing for them.
The soft rains
I sing for them.
The little winds
I sing for them.
I sing for them.

The Song of the Summer Bird

All is beautiful
    before me
    behind me
    around me
    everywhere.
All is beautiful.

The Song of the Autumn Bird

Hear my power.
I make the east wind come and
         pass over the ground.
I sing in the mountains.
I sing among the rocks.
I sing to the morning stars.
Hear my power.

The fisher and the wolf set the beautiful singing
birds free. 'Fly to earth,' said the fisher.
'Sing your songs of spring, summer and autumn
down below where it is winter all the year round.'
The birds flew over the plain, and through the
hole in the sky, down to the earth beneath.

But the Thunderers were returning home
to their lodges. When they saw the empty
cages, they took up their bows and arrows
and ran across the plain. They ran to try
and catch the fisher and the wolf, who
had stolen their singing birds.

The wolf was first through the hole, but the fisher was slower. An arrow hit his tail and he died. His body stretched across the hole in the sky, so no Thunderer can ever come down to earth. And no bird of spring, summer or autumn can ever return to the land above.

The weather on earth became warmer.
As season followed season the wolf's son
recovered and was strong. The fisher's
body turned into stars. Many times the
wolf sat and watched them twinkling.
Many times he told his son the story of
his friend's bravery, and how they brought
the birds of spring, summer and autumn
to earth.